VALENTINE FOR A DRAGON

VALENTINE
FOR A DRAGON

by Shirley Rousseau Murphy

Illustrated by Kay Chorao

ATHENEUM   1984   NEW YORK

Library of Congress Cataloging in Publication Data

Murphy, Shirley Rousseau.
Valentine for a dragon.

Summary: A demon thinks of a special gift to win the love of a
lady dragon on Valentine's Day.
[1. Valentine's Day—Fiction.   2. Dragons—Fiction.   3. Devil—
Fiction]   I. Chorao, Kay, ill.   II. Title.
PZ7.M956Val   1984   [E]   83-17911
ISBN 0-689-31016-1

Published simultaneously in Canada by
McClelland & Stewart, Ltd.
Composition by Dix Type Inc., Syracuse, New York
Printed and bound by Halliday Lithograph Corporation,
West Hanover, Massachusetts
Typography by Mary Ahern
First Edition

For Kori, Alicia and Geig

nce in a time of wonders a demon loved a dragon, but the dragon did not love him in return. She didn't know he existed.

She was a fine dragon, immense and silvery. She lived in the mountain beyond the village.

The demon was a shy, plain little fellow, who lived in a cottage at the edge of the village and tried not to offend anyone.

The dragon had breath like flaming volcanoes, so bright she could light up the whole countryside at night. Her voice was louder than a hundred trombones and a thousand kettle drums, so people covered their ears when she bellowed, and all the glasses on all the shelves in all the houses cracked into splinters. Her smoky breath left cinders hanging in the sky for days, spoiling everyone's laundry. The townspeople hated having a dragon so near. They complained of her fiery soot and of her thunder.

They didn't like having the demon near, either.
They said *he* was too different. Too small, too
funny-looking. Too strange to suit them, with his
little spells for exotic cookery—which were the
only spells he remembered properly from demon
school—and his eccentric ways. They scowled at
him when they passed him on the street, and they
would not walk by his little house. They never
invited him to parties. When he came into the
shops, they would say, "There's that demon again!
He oughtn't be allowed in the village. He oughtn't
be allowed among real folk!"

When the demon heard their whispers, he
would cry the rest of the day. "They are hateful!"
he would sob. Then, "*I* don't care! I don't care a
whit about them!"

But he cared for the dragon; he loved her to
distraction, longed for her night and day. If the
dragon loved him, he knew he would not feel
lonely. Still he was far too bashful to go up the
mountain to her den, too shy ever to speak to her.
"If only she knew I was alive! If only she could love
me, I would be happy forever."

She was so beautiful, so shiny silver, so broad
of wing, such fiery breath. While he was dull and
insignificant.

The demon grew lonelier and more desperate. And, as is sometimes the way with desperation, at last he had an idea.

Oh, it would take courage. All the courage he could muster.

He would give her a valentine. There were rows of them in the little shop, and tomorrow was Valentine's Day. He would find the most beautiful one and take it to the dragon, put aside his bashful shyness, and present it to her. The boldness of the idea made him quiver. But with such a gift, the dragon would surely love him.

He took all his savings out of the sugar bowl. He bought a new suit of clothes to look presentable in, blue serge, with a pale orange shirt and a fine necktie. Then he purchased the biggest, fanciest valentine the shop had to offer. It was covered with lace and red satin and flowers and hearts and little birds. No dragon could resist it. He wrote across the front of it, in his best penmanship that he had learned at demon school, "To Fervicent, the most wonderful dragon in the world."

Early in the morning on Valentine's Day, he carried the valentine up the mountain to Fervicent's cave, and he knocked, and he waited with shuffling feet.

Fervicent looked out.

She was a marvelous dragon. She had teeth like Japanese swords, claws like scythes, and ears as warty as a hog's hide. She bent way down to look at the demon.

She peered at him with one eye, then turned her head and peered with the other. Then she said, with a voice as hot as if you'd opened the oven door, "Well, what do you want, demon? I never in my life saw such a little, tiny, puny demon as you."

The demon blushed with embarrassment. "I want—I want—I want to give. . . ." He held the valentine out. He nearly fainted of shyness and of love for the wonderful dragon. He hiccupped once, then dropped the valentine under her chin, and fled.

When he got to a safe distance, where she would not see his blushes, he peered around a rock. Would she like his valentine? Would she be impressed by it?

The dragon watched the demon run away, and she didn't see the valentine there beneath her chin. "Now why," she said, little flames spurting out of the corners of her mouth, "why was that demon knocking on my door?" And of course when she spoke, her fiery breath burned the valentine to cinders.

When she glanced down at last and noticed the pile of ashes, she was quite puzzled. "Now why in the world . . ." she muttered, "why would anyone bring me a pile of ashes? Does that demon think I have no ashes of my own? Why my cave is full of ashes! The ashes of peasants, the ashes of oxen and knights and even a king or two! What do I need with this little clawful of fluff!"

The demon went home and cried for a long time for the end of his lovely valentine and his failure with the dragon.

Then he sat wiping his tears and sniffing.

Then he began to think.

What kind of present *can* you give a dragon? Paper was surely no good; he could not give her picture postcards or writing paper, they would all burn up. He gazed out at the hillside where the first spring flowers were blooming. He could not give her a calendar or a book to read or a box of tissue to wipe her smoky nose. Oh dear.

Then suddenly he knew what he could give her, and he raced out onto the hills.

He gathered a great armload of crocuses and jonquils and narcissus, and put a ribbon around them. And he hied himself off to the dragon. He knocked on her door, then stood staring up at her, quite overcome again with love and shyness. "I want . . . I'd like to give. . . ." He gulped twice with embarrassment and self-consciousness, dropped the flowers under her chin, and fled. Then he stood watching from behind a rock, as before.

Fervicent looked down to see what *this* was, and her breath scorched the poor flowers into a mass of brown, withered straw.

"Whatever is the matter with that fellow? Does he think I need a pile of straw? I would rather . . ." she said softly and mournfully, ". . . I would rather have someone to talk to. It gets lonely being a dragon. Especially on Valentine's Day." She snorted with unhappiness. "Today is Valentine's Day, and I am all alone, and all that demon can think to do is bring me ashes and straw."

The demon didn't hear her. He was crying too loudly. He went home depressed, sure his love would never be fulfilled. Everything he gave her ended up straw and ashes. After a while, though, he dried his tears and thought that maybe a little breakfast would make him feel better.

He had no butter or eggs, so he dug his last few pennies out of the sugar bowl and went to the village shop. It was half full of people, shopping for Valentine's Day. He heard someone whisper behind his back, "There's that demon! Did you see him running up the mountain this morning? What's he up to *now?*"

Someone whispered back, "I saw him carrying flowers and the biggest valentine in town up the mountain. There's nothing up there but that dragon. Surely the demon is quite mad."

"He's peculiar, all right. Don't let anyone tell him about our valentine party. We don't want *him* there."

"Oh, I won't tell. We don't want that demon at the party."

The demon heard the whispers, and he went home and cried about that. Then, finished crying at last, he began to make himself some pancakes. Flour. Butter. Eggs. Sugar—and when he opened the cupboard to reach for the sugar, he had an idea.

Oh, a wonderful idea.

Such an idea that he could hardly contain himself. He danced around the kitchen, then fetched down the sugar, then the chocolate, and began to mix and stir. He would make a present that would certainly delight the dragon. A present that could never turn to straw or to ashes.

Surely the dragon would love rich chocolate fudge with walnuts. In demon school he had been famous for his fudge with walnuts. He mixed and cooked and beat, and by noon he had the loveliest batch of fudge any dragon ever laid a lip over. He tied the plate with a ribbon and started off up the mountain as fast as his little legs would carry him.

The demon knocked on the dragon's door, and now he was feeling bolder. When the dragon stuck her head out, he held the plate right up to her, and she bent to look. He shivered ever so slightly at the thrill of her closeness.

She looked at the plate with one eye, then she turned her head and looked with the other. Then she bent her head to sniff the wonderful smell. And of course her scorching breath melted the fudge into a stream of chocolate that ran right off the plate and all over the demon's new suit.

The demon fled, stricken.

His lovely fudge was ruined. His new suit was ruined, to say nothing of his orange shirt and fine tie. And worst of all, he had failed for the third time. Everyone knows that the third failure is the final, ignoble failure. He trudged away home with tears pouring down to mix with the rivers of chocolate across his serge lapels.

Fervicent stared after him. Then she bent and began to lap up the good hot chocolate the little demon had left her. "Buy why . . ." she said, licking the plate clean, then licking her warty lips, ". . . why did he bring hot chocolate on a *plate*? Everyone knows hot chocolate is served in a mug!"

Meanwhile, poor demon sat on his doorstep and cried up such a storm that he could be heard all over town. People said, "What's the matter with that demon?"

"*I* don't know. I haven't time to worry about him! I'm making favors for the party!"

"Well I do wish he'd be still. He's going to spoil the whole party if he keeps *that* up. We won't be able to hear the music or enjoy ourselves at all. Why must he carry on so on Valentine's Day! Can't he wait till tomorrow!"

And another said, "The sky is darkening to rain. That's probably the demon's fault, too."

"He's a thoughtless, horrible little demon. It would be just like him to make it rain and spoil our party. I wish he were gone from here! I wish that demon were dead!"

Their voices were loud. They reached the poor demon easily, there on his front porch. Oh, this was the very last straw. Not only did the dragon not love him, but everyone else hated him, too. He felt terrible.

He felt so bad he decided he would do away with himself. "I'll get myself dead, just the way they'd like, and *then* they'll be sorry! When it's too late, they'll be sorry, and that will serve them right." He sobbed and hiccupped. "I'll go up in the hills right now, before it rains." The sky surely was beginning to darken. "I'll dig my grave up in the hills and carve my headstone saying, *Here lies a demon dead because no one loved him,* and I'll get myself dead in the pouring rain and then they'll be sorry." He took up a shovel, and a chisel for carving his headstone, and started off toward the hills.

When he got to a suitable hilltop, bare and lonely beneath a darkened sky and just right for his grave, the demon began to dig.

The clouds grew thicker and lower. The ground was rocky and hard and seemed to grow harder. The shovel was dull and grew duller. Soon the demon was very tired of digging. His back ached. His arms hurt. Did he really want to die of unrequited love in this empty place and lie here alone forever?

He stopped digging and sat down on a stone to think.

Pretty soon the wind turned so chill he
gathered twigs and built a little fire to warm
himself. No sense dying cold and uncomfortable.

A few drops of rain began to fall. He propped
his shovel on a forked stick to protect the fire. The
wind grew colder still, and the demon was getting
hungry. No use to die hungry and wet.

Soon all the glamour of dying had left him. He
wondered why he had come up here. He picked up
his shovel and his chisel and threw a handful of
gravel on the fire to put it out. He would go home
and have supper and be lonely where it was warm
and comfortable.

But what was this? The gravel didn't put the fire out, it made it blaze higher. And the flames turned to bright blue, then to green. The demon stared, amazed.

He threw on another handful of gravel.

A green flame shot up.

He found more gravel, threw it on, and watched blue flame burst forth bright as jewels. He stood looking, puzzled and interested.

Then at last he understood. Why, he had learned about this in demon school. He tried to remember the lesson.

At last, and very slowly, he began to recall the spell.

> *"Find your rocks and pound them fine,*
> *And throw them on the flame.*
> *Copper for green,*
> *Tellurium for blue,*
> *And—and . . ."*

But he could remember no more. He stood looking at the gravel in his hand. There was a whole spell about how to make colors, if he could only remember it. Why, he could make rainbows in the fire.

But then he thought, what good would that do? He hadn't come up here to make fancy colors. How could that make the dragon love him, or the people in the village either?

Still, he repeated the spell, pondering. "Copper for green, tellurium for blue, and—and strontium for red!"

And then he began to have an idea.

While the demon's idea was exploding in his mind, over on the mountain the dragon had been awakened by the rain. She heard the pattering and came to her door to look. Then, peering out, she heard cries in the village below, and she slithered out farther to see what was going on.

The rain felt good on her snout. She licked some up, then stretched out full length in the downpour and stared down at the village below. She thought they must be having a party down there, with all the decorations. But why was everyone running about dragging tables and chairs back inside the houses?

Maybe people didn't like rain. Maybe it spoiled their party. She sat looking down longingly at the village. No one had invited her to a party. She saw red paper hearts hung from trees. They were limp with rain. Had it been a Valentine's party? Oh, she wished she had been asked. She sat staring down forlornly, awash with loneliness.

And then she thought, what would happen if she invited herself to the party? What would happen if she just crept down there quietly and asked to join in?

She could hold her breath so flames would not spurt on folks. She would not roar, she would ask in a whisper, and politely. The dragon sat pondering this, then she got up and started down the mountain, longing with all her heart to join the fun.

Meanwhile, where was the demon?

The little demon came down the hills through the rain, meaning to go right through the village and up the mountain to the dragon's den, with his wonderful new gift for Fervicent. He was giddy with anticipation. He would give her the copper ore and the tellurium, and some strontium, too. He would show her how to make magnificent colored flames. He had removed his orange shirt and wrapped quantities of the gravel up in it. Oh, this gift would not turn to ashes or straw, or melt and run all over him.

But in the village his progress was hindered by
folk running this way and that dragging party
decorations out of the rain, by women running
indoors with cakes and bunting flags, as the rain
pelted down, soaking tablecloths and colored
streamers and washing away food. The voices of the
townsfolk were distraught.

"Save the cookies! Rescue the sandwiches!"
"The lemonade is running over the pitcher!"
The hearts on the bandstand were bleeding red
dye, a little girl's dress had shrunk up around her
armpits, and limp doilies were floating in the
gutter.
"The band has gone home!"
"Oh, the party is ruined!"
And then someone saw the dragon.

"The dragon is coming! The dragon!"

"Run! Save my child!"

"Hide in the cellar!"

Fervicent slid quietly down the mountain and into the village. Those folk who had not escaped stood frozen with fear at her approach.

Only the demon was not afraid. He stood wondering. Why was the dragon coming here? What did she mean to do? Had the unkindness of the village maddened her at last? Did she mean to destroy the village while folk were too distraught and confused to defend themselves?

The demon thought she did. He took heart and grew braver and cheered her. "On, dragon! On, dragon! Wipe the village flat!"

The dragon came closer. The few remaining folk disappeared into doorways. The street stood empty, except for soggy party tables, wet cakes, and fading flags. The rain drizzled dishearteningly.

The dragon stopped in the center of the village. Her scales were shiny wet. She was woozy from holding her breath so as not to breathe flame on the townsfolk. Everyone had fled except the little demon, there in the middle of the street. She felt better knowing someone was not afraid of her, felt warmed inside.

She saw the ruins of the party. Saw the soggy mess the rain had made. Saw folk peering out fearfully through their windows.

And she knew what she would do.

Fervicent reared to her full height above the village. She reared taller than trees, far taller than the church steeple. She opened her mouth wide enough to swallow a house. She breathed out a flame of fire so huge it covered the sky.

A canopy of flame hung above the village, whipping in the wind.

Rain hissed down onto the flames and disappeared into steam. No rain drop fell, now, onto tables and cakes. The village turned as warm and bright as summer beneath her fiery breath.

The cakes began to dry, though their icing
melted. The paper plates dried, slightly singed. The
flowers and the bunting tablecloths dried. The rain
pattered all around on the hills, but it did not touch
the village. Fervicent's hot breath licked across the
sky as Fervicent reared towering, and soon
everything beneath her was warm and dry.

Folk began to come out.

They dried themselves in her warmth.

The demon cut a slice of cake, took up a
sandwich, and smiled shyly up at the dragon.

The orchestra came out, holding their trombones and zithers up to the heat so Fervicent could dry them.

The children came, basking in her warmth, staring up at her flame as one would stare at a wonderful sunset. They cut cake and took sandwiches and poured out hot lemonade that tasted different and new.

The party became happy with music and eating and drinking and merriment and the dancing of reels and clogs. And Fervicent kept back the rain with her flames until, at last, the rain clouds, disheartened, drifted far away. It was then the demon stepped close to the dragon, though still his shyness made him tongue-tied. He held out his shirt made into a package, then poured from it onto the ground a little pile of copper ore, a little pile of tellurium, and one of strontium.

Fervicent glanced down, then looked at the demon, puzzled anew. What now? What strange present was this? First ashes, then straw, then hot chocolate on a plate. Now what was this? Piles of rock?

All around them, the village folk had stopped dancing and singing to watch. What was the demon up to now?

At last the demon found his tongue. "Breathe on them," he whispered. "Blow flame on them. They're—it's a gift."

The dragon cocked her head and stared with one eye at the little piles of gravel.

"Breathe!" urged the demon more boldly.

She breathed out a small lick of flame onto the copper ore.

The ore flared up bright blue, beautiful as butterflies. The dragon stared in amazement.

Then she breathed again, a fiery sigh onto the tellurium. Flame shot up green as emeralds. The dragon gaped, then smiled with delight. Never in all her life had her breath been so beautiful. Like flowers and rare jewels. She breathed again, and again the colors flared. Again. She smiled. Again. Flames danced cerulean and turquoise and azure. She breathed on the strontium, and the flames danced red. Again, again, until at last the little piles of ore were all used up.

"I have more," whispered the demon, showing her his tied-up shirt. "I can get more and more, all you will ever want."

The dragon knelt. She kissed the demon on the forehead. He was a wonderful small demon. She took him on her back very gently, lifting him in her sword-sharp teeth just in the center of his collar.

Together they joined the party.

The demon and the dragon together stuffed on cake and hot lemonade and sandwiches until nightfall. And then the dragon made fireworks for the party. She coughed up cascades of blue and red and green and turquoise fire in the shape of hearts and birds and all the wonders of a summer meadow. She delighted the children and made their parents smile with awe.

And when the party was ended, the dragon and the demon went away. To make a new life. They lived for hundreds of years, and nevermore were they parted. They took slithering gallops across the stony mountains. They were always warm in the dragon's bright flame, always well fed with the demon's cooking that he had learned in demon school. And every Valentine's Day the dragon made hearts of red fire and blue, written on the sky to show her affection for the demon. And the demon made fudge for her and brought her flowers and valentines. She never scorched one again, not ever. And neither of them was, again, ever lonely.

And in the village, for hundreds of years, folk loved dragons. And they loved demons. And they let each creature live as it chose.